MY
Christmas Wonderland

Brown Watson
ENGLAND

Printed in Hungary.

KU-130-597

Contents

© 1990 Brown Watson (Leicester) Ltd.

The Fancy Dress Parade

Nice things always seem to be happening around Christmas-time, don't they? But, for Tom and Jane, there's an extra treat this year! They have just heard that there is to be a Christmas Fancy Dress Parade followed by a carol concert at the shopping precinct, with all the children taking part! The idea is to raise money for people in hospital.

"I'm going as Santa Claus!" says Tom at once. "I've got my red pyjamas at home, Jane, and there's the red bobble hat Mummy knitted. All I need is a cotton wool beard!" Jane starts to laugh, thinking of her brother as Santa Claus. "What about me as the fairy on the Christmas tree?" she cries.

She is already thinking of a lovely, white frilly dress with a star in her hair as they wait their turn to tell Miss Nelson what they want to be.

"So, Tom's going as Santa Claus," she smiles, writing in her book. "Who's next?"

"I want to go as a fairy," says Sara, Jane's friend.

"Ah, yes," says Miss Nelson, smiling again. "You were a bridesmaid only a little while ago, weren't you? Your dress is much too pretty to wear it only once."

Poor Jane! She doesn't like to say she wanted to be a fairy, too.

"Never mind, Jane," whispers Tom. "We'll think of something else."

"What about Christmas Holly?" suggests Mummy when they tell her what has happened. "You could have a nice, new green dress trimmed with some red berries and ribbon!"

"Holly Turner's thought of that," says Jane in a small voice, seeing Tom getting started on his Santa Claus costume. "And Miss Nelson said she's got the right name!"

Then, Daddy thinks of an idea.

"Borrow my bathrobe, Jane," he says. "Then you could go as a snowman!"

"Or a Christmas angel!" adds Tom, trying to be helpful. Even Muffin wags his tail!

"I think your robe might be a bit too big for Jane to wear," smiles Mummy. And Jane has to agree . . . .

Nobody else has any problems choosing their Fancy Dress! Tom is the perfect Santa Claus, Sara is the Christmas fairy, Holly wears her holly dress and Lucy makes a lovely Christmas tree! Tom's friend, Jason is a shepherd, Darren is a carol singer – and Laura's costume is the most wonderful Christmas cracker!

"Don't worry, Jane," says Miss Nelson. "Just think of all the good things of Christmas, and you're sure to get an idea for the Fancy Dress Parade!"

"All the good things of Christmas . . . ." Jane repeats, almost in a whisper. Miss Nelson's words set her thinking again. "All the good things of Christmas . . . ."

The minute she gets home, Jane tells Mummy what Miss Nelson has said.

"Fetch your painting overall," says Mummy, "and I'll start making lots of pockets to stitch on it."

And whilst she's busy, Tom and Jane set to work.

Tom makes a pretend Christmas pudding, and Jane wraps up an empty box to make it look like a Christmas tree parcel! Then they cut out pictures of all the Christmassy things they can find from old Christmas cards and wrapping paper. Mummy says she wants enough for something to go in each of the pockets.

"I'm the Good Things of Christmas!" laughs Jane. How proud she is when a nurse asks her to stand by the Christmas tree to help collect money for the hospital!
Everyone in the shopping precinct stops to look – and soon it seems that the people in hospital will have lots of good things for Christmas! Tom and Jane certainly hope so!

The Twelve Days of Christmas

On the twelfth day of Christmas,
My true love sent to me –
Twelve drummers drumming,
Eleven pipers piping,
Ten lords a-leaping,
Nine ladies dancing,
Eight maids a-milking,
Seven swans a-swimming,
Six geese a-laying,
Five gold rings,
Four calling birds,
Three French hens,
Two turtle doves,
And a partridge in a pear tree.

The Christmas Tree

Tom and Jane always like helping Mummy and Daddy to put up the Christmas decorations. They both agree that the nicest part comes when Daddy switches on the fairy lights on their Christmas tree!
"Christmas Lighting-Up Time," he always calls it, with everyone standing by to see how lovely the tree looks.

But, this year – the lights just flicker, and then go out again. Daddy checks the switch, then looks at all the lights. Tom and Jane try not to worry. They remember the same thing happening last year, then Daddy fixed the lights and made them work. Maybe he can mend them again.

Daddy tries his best, but it's no good. "We'll have to throw these away," he says. Tom and Jane are so disappointed. Now, it's too late to go out and buy some new lights – the shops are all closed!
"Never mind," smiles Mummy. "We'll hang some Christmas chocolates on the tree, and make it look just as nice, tomorrow!"

Tom and Jane aren't really sure about that . . . . But, next morning, Mummy is still smiling.
"Something nice for the Christmas tree!" she cries.
But there are no fairy lights in her basket – only a handful of drinking straws, some cotton, a few bits of kitchen foil . . . . and a packet of macaroni!
"Fetch your paints, Jane!" she says.

Soon, Jane is painting macaroni, ready to thread on to cotton and hang from the tree! Mummy shows Tom how to cut the drinking straws into small pieces, then tie them together in the middle to make Christmas stars! As for Muffin – he thinks scrunching up the foil to make silver balls is great fun!

Later on, they make what Mummy calls "Cracker Candies" by wrapping sweets in strips of gift-wrap. "Tie them at each end, then cut the edges," she says. "They'll look like tiny Christmas Crackers!" And that's just what everyone thinks when they call in and see the Christmas tree!

16

"Merry Christmas!" cry Tom and Jane, when their friends come around and see their lovely Christmas tree, with Cracker Candies for everyone! Tom and Jane can see they'll soon be none left – but they don't mind one bit! They know they can make lots more for all their Christmas visitors!

A Visit from St. Nicholas

'Twas the night before Christmas, when all through the house
Not a creature was stirring, not even a mouse;
The stockings were hung by the chimney with care,
In hopes that St. Nicholas soon would be there.

The children were nestled all snug in their beds,
While visions of sugarplums danced in their heads;
And mamma in her kerchief, and I in my cap,
Had just settled our brains for a long winter nap;

When out on the lawn there arose such a clatter,
I sprang from my bed to see what was the matter.
Away to the window I flew like a flash,
Tore open the shutters and threw up the sash.

The moon, on the breast of the new-fallen snow,
Gave lustre of midday to objects below,
When, what to my wondering eyes should appear,
But a miniature sleigh and eight tiny reindeer

With a little old driver so lively and quick,
I knew in a moment it must be St. Nick.
More rapid than eagles, his coursers they came,
And he whistled and shouted and called them by name:

"Now, Dasher! now, Dancer! now, Prancer and Vixen!
'On Comet! on Cupid! on Donner and Blitzen!
To the top of the porch, to the top of the wall,
Now, dash away! dash away! dash away all!"

As dry leaves that before the wild hurricane fly,
When they meet with an obstacle, mount to the sky,
So up to the housetop the coursers they flew,
With the sleigh full of toys, and St. Nicholas, too.

And then, in a twinkling, I heard on the roof
The prancing and pawing of each little hoof.
As I drew in my head, and was turning around,
Down the chimney St. Nicholas came with a bound.

He was dressed all in fur from his head to his foot,
And his clothes were all tarnished with ashes and soot;
A bundle of toys he had flung on his back,
And he looked like a pedlar just opening his pack.

His eyes – how they twinkled! His dimples – how merry!
His cheeks were like roses, his nose like a cherry.
His droll little mouth was drawn up like a bow,
And the beard on his chin was as white as the snow.

The stump of a pipe he held tight in his teeth,
And the smoke it encircled his head like a wreath.
He had a broad face and a little round belly
That shook when he laughed like a bowlful of jelly.

He was chubby and plump, a right jolly old elf,
And I laughed when I saw him in spite of myself.
A wink of his eye and a twist of his head
Soon gave me to know I had nothing to dread.

He spoke not a word, but went straight to his work,
And filled all the stockings; then turned with a jerk,
And laying his finger aside of his nose,
And giving a nod, up the chimney he rose.

He sprang to his sleigh, to his team gave a whistle
And away they all flew like the down of a thistle.
But I heard him exclaim, 'ere he drove out of sight,
"Happy Christmas to all, and to all a good night!"

My Snowman Friend

I call him Mr. Frosty-Face!
He brings us so much fun,
With his black coal eyes, and carrot nose,
And a smile for everyone!

If we play Ring-a-Roses,
Then all our friends join in!
But, when the game is "Statues",
He always knows he'll win!

When I talk, I know he'll listen
To every word I say.
I can shout, or knock his hat off,
And he'll never run away!

But, when the weather's warmer,
Then Frosty-Face must go –
Until the next time that he comes
With winter's ice and snow.

The Christmas Present

Tom and Jane are in town window-shopping,
today. Lots of people are there, getting all sorts
of things for Christmas. Tom and Jane want to
buy a present for Mummy.
"We don't want something she's got already,"
says Jane. "What about a Christmas
decoration for the table like that one?"
"We haven't got enough money!"
Tom tells her.

Daddy thinks Tom and Jane would like some mince pies and a milk shake at the café. Mummy is already there with her friends, and they're all talking about what they want for Christmas.

"Finding my engagement ring would be enough for me!" sighs Mummy. "I've searched simply everywhere, but it seems I've lost it!"

Seeing Mummy so upset makes Tom and Jane feel very sad. They both helped her look for her ring, so they know how hard she searched.

"I wish we could buy her one of those Christmas decorations," sighs Jane.

"Maybe we can't buy one . . . ." says Tom slowly. "But I think we could make one! Come on, Jane, let's try!"

They put on their boots and their coats and dash out into the garden. Muffin soon brings Tom a piece of bark which flaked off a tree. "There were pine cones on the decoration we saw," he reminds Jane. "Can you find any?"

"Making Christmas decorations?" smiles Mrs. Jones next door. "You can have this holly I've just cut from my bush."

They cannot wait to get started! First, Tom cleans the bark with screwed-up newspaper, and puts a blob of plasticene in the middle. Then it's all ready to hold the spray of holly and the fir cones, with one of Jane's birthday candles in the centre!

"Let's make some paste with flour and water," says Tom. "Have we got any glitter?"

"To sprinkle on the paste and make it look like sparkly snow?" asks Jane in delight. But, before Tom can answer, Mummy comes in and gives a little scream.

"Tom! Just look at the mud on your boots!"

Oh, dear! Tom and Jane were so keen to begin making Mummy's present, they didn't bother about the mess they were making . . . .

But, Mummy isn't shouting about the mess on the floor. She has seen her engagement ring, stuck into a clod of earth underneath Tom's boot. She must have lost it in the garden!
"It's the best Christmas present I could have!" she smiles happily. Tom and Jane smile, too, thinking of the lovely Christmas decoration they have made for her.

Great Uncle Charles

Tom and Jane are having their Grandma staying with them for the Christmas holiday. She always has time to read them a story, play games, and see all their new toys . . . . But this year, Daddy says she is bringing Great Uncle Charles with her.

"Great Uncle Charles?" echoes Tom.

"Who is he, Daddy?" asks Jane.

"Granny's brother," explains Daddy. "And your Mummy's uncle. He has lived abroad for most of his life, and that's why you don't remember hearing about him."

Tom and Jane do not know quite what to think. They both start wondering what it will be like, having Great Uncle Charles to stay for Christmas . . . .

Great Uncle Charles reminds Tom of a soldier, the way he marches up the front path and calls out in a loud voice.

"Hello, hello! How lovely to see you all! And this is Tom and Jane? My, my, I can see I'll be kept busy this Christmas Eve, telling stories and roasting chestnuts around the fire!"

"We haven't any chestnuts," Tom points out.
"And there isn't any fire," adds Jane.
But they soon discover that nothing bothers their
Great Uncle Charles.
"Draw the curtains, Tom," he says. "And, Jane –
can you find me a Christmas candle?"
As well as telling them a story, Great Uncle
Charles makes shadow pictures too!

Tom and Jane enjoy every minute. Visiting so
many countries and far-off lands has made Great
Uncle Charles the most wonderful story-teller!
They hardly hear Mummy and Grandma coming
into the room with some tea and mince pies –
and some special candied chestnuts which Great
Uncle Charles brought as a treat!

Then, after tea, he puts a coin into a cup, pours flour on top and Tom and Jane help him to press it down as firmly as they can. Everyone watches as he turns it out on to a plate – and that's when the fun begins! "Now try slicing through the flour castle, without disturbing the coin!" he laughs.

"Whoever cuts the last slice, so that nobody can make a slice after them, wins the money!"
But nobody cares about winning or losing! Everyone shouts and laughs as they take it in turns to slice into the flour. Tom and Jane decide it is one of their favourite games!

31

When it really seems that nobody could possibly laugh or shout any more, Great Uncle Charles turns to Grandma. "Come along!" he says. "Let us show Tom and Jane some of our conjuring tricks!" They did not know their Grandma was even interested in magic or conjuring. But Great Uncle Charles soon shows how clever she is!

By now, Tom and Jane are beginning to feel so sleepy. But, for once, they do not mind. Going to bed will only make Christmas Day come all the quicker – a day when they will be able to see more of their dear Great Uncle Charles. They are so glad that he has come to stay with them.